DISNEY·PIXAR
BRAVE

A MOTHER'S LOVE

By Melissa Lagonegro

Illustrated by Maria Elena Naggi
and Studio IBOIX

Random House 🏠 New York

Princess Merida is late.

The royal family waits.

Merida's mother

is the queen.

The queen teaches Merida
how to be a princess.
She shows Merida
how to play the harp.
Merida is bored.

Merida wants

to play with her sword.

The queen tells Merida
she must marry
the son of a lord.

It is her job
as the princess.
Merida is mad!

Merida gets ready
to meet some lords' sons.
She wears a fancy gown.
The queen is proud.

Merida is sad.
She does not want
to get married.

The young lords
will shoot arrows
at a target.

The best shooter
will marry the princess.

Merida joins the game.

She is the best.

She wins!

Now no one
can marry Merida.
The queen is mad.

The queen wants Merida
to get married.
Merida says no.

She cuts
the family tapestry.

Merida runs away.
She meets a Witch.
She asks the Witch
to change the queen.

The Witch makes a cake
that holds a spell.
The spell
will change the queen.

Merida returns
to the castle.
The queen eats
the spell cake.

The cake
changes the queen—
into a bear!
Merida did not want this.

Merida and her mother
look for the Witch.
They need her
to break the spell.
But the Witch is gone!

Merida and her mother
go fishing.
They have fun.

Merida and her mother
meet a mean bear.
They run back
to the castle.

Merida wants
to help her mother.
She wants to mend
the family tapestry.

Merida tells the lords
she will marry
one of their sons.
The queen stops her.
She wants Merida
to be happy.

The men chase the queen
from the castle.

The queen is in trouble.
No one knows
she is the bear!
Merida protects her.

The mean bear returns!
The queen
protects Merida.
The two bears fight.

Merida fixes

the torn tapestry.

She and her mother hug.

The tapestry covers them.

The queen is
human again!
Love has
broken the spell.

Merida and the queen
will always be
mother and daughter.
Now they are friends,
too.